D0329247

Itchy, Itchy Chicken Pox

To Jordan
—G.M.

To Taylor Duffy and Austin Geary,
in hopes that this book will comfort them
if and when they see their first spots.
—B.L.

No part of this publication may be reproduced, stored in a retrieval system,
or transmitted in any form or by any means, electronic, mechanical, photocopying, recording
or otherwise, without written permission of the publisher. For information regarding permissi
write to Scholastic Inc., Attention: Permissions Department, 557 Broadway, New York, NY 100

Text copyright © 1992 by Grace Maccarone.
Illustration copyright © 1992 by Betsy Lewin.
Activities copyright © 2003 by Scholastic Inc.

All rights reserved. Published by Scholastic Inc.
SCHOLASTIC, CARTWHEEL BOOKS, and associated logos
are trademarks and/or registered trademarks of Scholastic Inc.

Library of Congress Cataloging-in-Publication Data is available.

ISBN: 0-590-44948-6

40 39 38 37 36   15 16 17 18/0

Printed in the U.S.A.   40
First printing, May 1992

Itchy, Itchy Chicken Pox

by Grace Maccarone
Illustrated by Betsy Lewin

SCHOLASTIC INC.

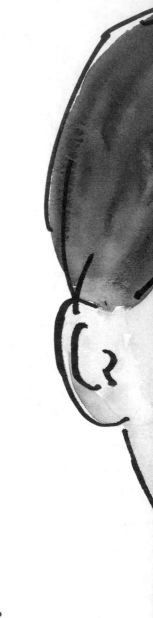

A spot.
A spot.
Another spot.

Uh-oh!
Chicken pox!

Under my shirt.
Under my socks.

Itchy, itchy
chicken pox.

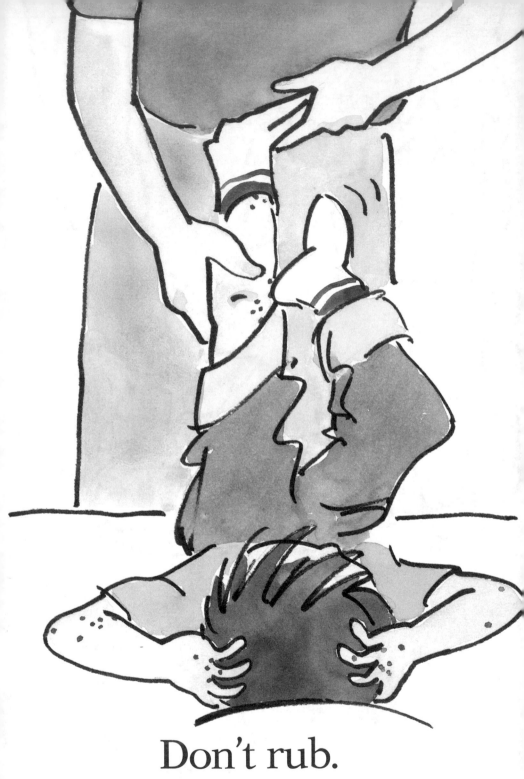

Don't rub.
Don't scratch.

Oh, no!
Another batch!

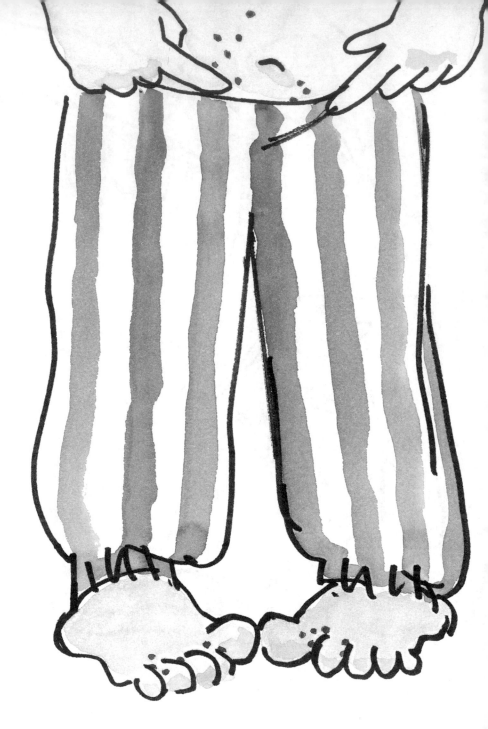

On my tummy,
between my toes,

down my back,
on my nose!

Lotion on.
Itching's gone
just for now.

It comes back—
OW!

One and two
and three and four.
Five and six…
and more and more.

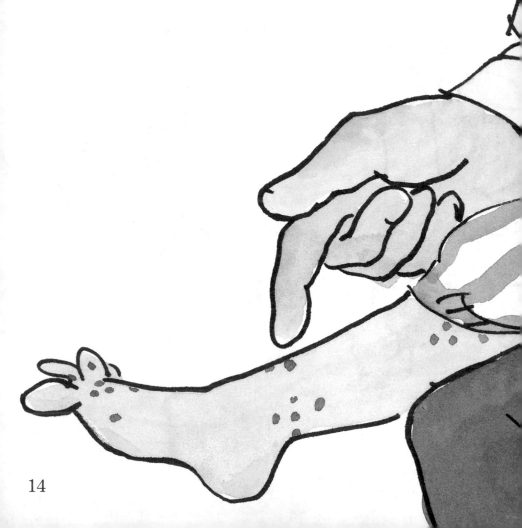

Daddy counts
my itchy spots.
Lots and lots
of chicken pox.

Itchy, itchy,
I feel twitchy....

I run away.
The itching stays.

Rubber ducky doesn't
like my yucky, mucky
oatmeal bath.
But Mommy says
it's good for me.

I rest.

I read.

I eat.

I play.

I feel better
every day.

And then…
no new spots.
Hooray!

I'm okay!
I get to go
to school today!